THE CURSED WOODS

KRITIKA K. GIRHEPUNJE

Made with ❤ on the Notion Press Platform
www.notionpress.com

To my family, who never stopped believing in me,
even when I doubted myself.

Contents

FOREWORD

Every once in a while, a story comes along that pulls you into a world you didn't know you needed—a world built not only with words, but with emotion, imagination, and truth.

This book is one of those rare journeys.

From the very first page, you'll be invited to see through the eyes of characters who feel as real as anyone you've ever known. You'll walk beside them, feel their hopes, their fears, their quiet triumphs—and perhaps, along the way, discover something new about yourself.

What makes this work especially remarkable is not just the story it tells, but the way it's told—with heart, courage, and an honest voice that stays with you long after you've finished the final chapter.

It's more than a story. It's an experience.

And now, it's yours.

— *Dr. Ranju Pal Girhepunje*

11ᵗʰ June, 2025

ACKNOWLEDGEMENTS

Writing this book has been a journey full of learning, growth and fun !! This book would not have been possible without the support, encouragement, and inspiration.

First and foremost, I want to thank my mother for her insightful feedback, steady guidance, and tireless commitment to bringing out the best in this manuscript. Your love, support, and encouragement kept me going, even on the hard days.

The next thanks goes to my father, for helping me with all the technical works required in the book like the pictures and all. You've taught me to stay strong, to keep going, and to believe in myself—even when things got tough.

A thank you for my younger brother for always making me smile and laugh. Your love, help, and belief in me meant a lot. Even in small ways, you showed me how to stay happy, strong, and not give up.

The last thanks goes to Ishika, Ishita, Janhvi and all my batchmates for always being by my side and helping me. Whether it was listening to my ideas, cheering me on, or simply making me smile when I needed it most—you helped me more than you know.

This book is a small reflection of the strength, laughter, and kindness I've found in your company. I'm truly grateful to have you in my life.

Finally, to my readers—thank you for your time, curiosity, and openness. It is for you that this book was written, and it is in your hands that it finds its true purpose.

With sincere appreciation,
Kritika

Prologue

They said the forest was cursed.

Whispers carried on the wind told tales of a soul that wandered beneath the ancient trees—a soul twisted by darkness, cursed to remain until vengeance was fulfilled. Children were warned to stay away. Elders lowered their voices when they spoke its name.

But the truth was far more complicated.

On a pale autumn evening, as dusk melted into shadow, two girls stepped beyond the forest's edge—drawn by something they couldn't explain. It was not fear that called them, but a presence. A pulse. A silent cry buried deep in the earth, heard only by hearts still unclouded by fear.

They didn't know it then, but they had been chosen.

Not to destroy the soul.

Not to run from it.

But to understand it.

And to free it.

What had been mistaken for evil was only sorrow wrapped in myth.

A demon once pure, now forgotten by time.

A soul that had waited, not for vengeance—but for salvation.

And in the darkness of the forest, the truth would awaken.

I

Yur's homecoming

Her name was Yur. She was my aunt's daughter, who used to live not far away, in the town of Ravenclon. Her parents used to be busy all time, therefore they couldn't look after her. They even could not be with her on the sundays. I mean, most of the children, including me have not experienced it, but I'm sure, she must feel lonely. By the time she woke up, her parents would have left for work and they used to be back after she slept. Only saturday evenings were free for them. Yur usually said that she needs someone to take care of her, someone to play with her as she spent her day such that after coming from school, she had to attend classes. Later she had nothing to be done. One saturday evening, she told her parents that she would be alone everyday and she needed to be taken care of. Her parents said, "Well, we'll think about it and let you know by tomorrow, as we're coming home early tomorrow because of the local holiday." She expected, that her parents would get another job for her, unaware of what's going to happen next. The other day, when her parents arrived home, she asked them, "Mom, dad, are you leaving the job for me?" when aunt said, "*Nahi* kiddo, we're not. Instead we'll change your school." Hearing this Yur got even bewildered. She looked at her dad. Her facial expression were as if a question mark had appeared on her face. "But, changing the school won't change anything else. Will it?" "Yes it will." answered aunt.

"You're going to live at your grandparents' home, with Mrunda. From there you go to school with her, and be back to the house. Don't worry, we will, surely, keep visiting you." joined uncle. Yur was quite happy to know this, but she was a bit downhearted to leave home. It was not as if she was leaving it forever, but you know. We usually used to hang out when we were together. Yur, after a week, came to my house. Her parents stayed for a while. We had some fun together. Like my parents, uncle and aunt, and us. We played a match of UNO, and nani packed some chaklis, and ladoos she had make for Diwali coming up, for uncle and aunt to take home. Then, her parents talked to her for a bit, telling her to listen to my parents and grandparents', take care of herself, eat well and study well. the moment they left, Yur started crying. Everyone came running outside to see what was up, and saw Yur crying, so started calming Yur down, when I had an idea to watch a movie. I grabbed her wrist and took her with me upstairs. I asked her which film are we watcing? "The Smile" she said weeping. We sat the whole afternoon watch the film. In the evening, we thought of going to the park with nani. She took us there, and sat on a bench. We went away to play. after a lot of running and chasing, we were exhasted, and so we went to nani, and sat near her. I asked nani to tell us a story. As usual, its always our grandparents who have a bag full of stories to tell us, isn't it? So she asked us what story would we like to listen to, so Yur looked around and randomly pointed towards the forest near the park's boundry.

Rayli forest

It was a quite eerie forest, and so I also had the curiosity to know about the forest. She looked at the forest, and... The smile on her face faded. she started " Oh, that? that forest, um It-it is the *Rayli forest*. No one should go near it, especially in Diwali times. They say, there's a door on the ground covered with mud, if one goes there, they need to find the door, put the badge on it to open it-" "What kindi of badge nani?" Yur interrupted. "No one knows. Its just that the badge has to be put, the door opens. No one knows how it looks from inside, but it is said, there lives a demon in it. Surprisingly, the demon is a devotee of lord Rama. Every Diwali, she performs a ritual, and is not in the cave. She keeps roaming in the forest. Which is why it is dangerous to walk around the forest during the times of diwali." "Come on maa, kids, dinner is ready!" we hear mother call us. We stood up and started to move forward. Yur turned around and eyed the forest until I asked her if everything was fine. She said it was, but you know, I could read her curious face. She, without a doubt wanted to explore. I did not mind asking her about it. Anyways, at the dinner, mum, out of nowhere got to know that nani was telling us the *Rayli forest* thing. And so she asked nani to not tell us about it. After the dinner, we went in my room, and started talking about random things, and told each other our routine, and she told me about her school (aka my new school). That night was sleepless. Luckily it was friday, so we did not have to worry about waking up for school the very next day. We quickly took the laptop and turned it on. To be honest, no single one was aware that we were awake this late. The creepiest thing we found on the internet! We shivered as hard as we could. Listen, we looked at every single map of Ravenclon available, but we did not find the *Rayli forest* in even one of them. Things started getting stranger. We just read an article, a group of fifteen people going there, but never coming back! I mean, what would have even happened? We found an even creepier story. "*Chalo Mrunda*, read it" Yur asked me to read it, hiding behind a pillow. As I started reading the first few letters of the article, "Based on a true story." A shiver ran down my spine. True story? I tought as I continued reading, "Back ago, a guy named ----------- he had a normal job, and a mother to take care of- in the hospital. His mother was severly ill. A day, he was late for Office, and the road he employed was full of traffic, so he thought of using the forest route. Here, he walked a few steps, where they found his bag fallen down on the ground. What might have happened to him? No one knows. Police officers found-" "No Mrunda, wait! Don't tell me such scary things! I won't be able to sleep then!" Yur barged in. In effect, Yur is afraid of such things, especially if they are based on a real incident. I saved the link in a word document, so that i can read it when I am alone. We shut down the laptop, put it in it's place, and softly slipped in the blankets. It was 1 AM, and we were still not able to sleep. The curiosity to know what happened next had been killing me. I demanded that Yur and I should really read what's up next. Ig Yur might have felt sorry for reading the article ahead with me. The moment I asked her this, She made her face as if she wanted to say, are you crazy? And I said, "Yur, please?" She continuosly nodded no, but somehow I grabbed her hand and made her sit down on the chair beside me to read what came off next. I got the laptop and... I opened the word document and... I clicked on the link, and... "**SORRY, INVALID LINK. PLEASE RE -CHECK THE LINK AND TRY AGAIN:("**

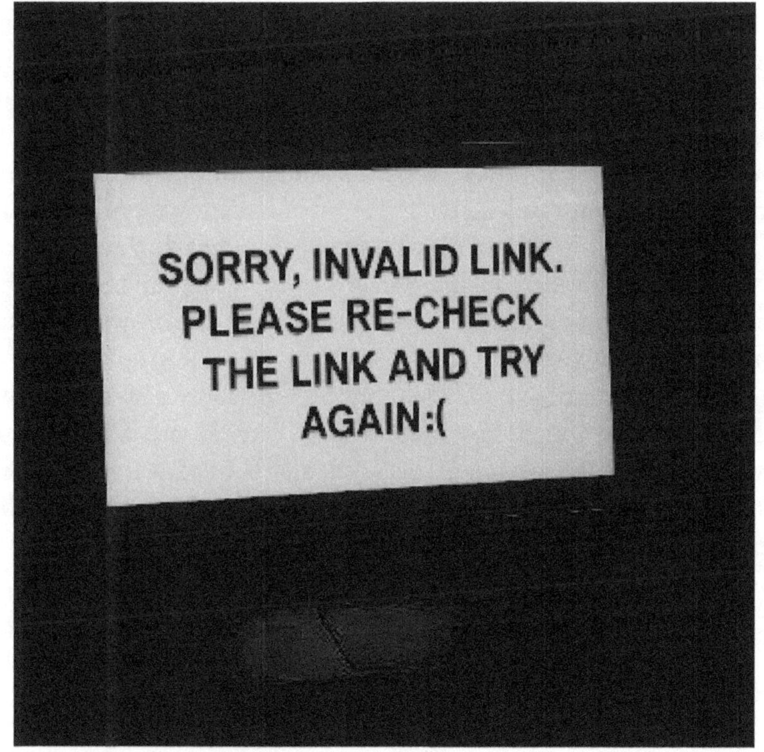

Laptop screen, when I actually wanted to read ahead

Written in Bold black letters. And I was like, why! Why! Why! Why! Why does it have to happen when needed?? I wiped my face with the hand, and was like, if not this time, I'll throw this laptop. I closed my eyes and clicked on the link. And again! It was The same page, the one with sorry. I turned around and looked at Yur. She shrugged and said, "Mrunda, we can do nothing but sleep. Shut down the laptop." Moreover, as I turned around to shut it down, the screen had the article. I jumped in happiness and started reading ahead. "Police officers found half of his body lying on the ground..." and I stopped. That was enough. We had been agitated as of reading this. I shut down the laptop. We went to the bed, and still after being tired the whole day, could not sleep. That was horrible. But once again to remind, it was friday night, so no worries. Next morning, (Ya, no waking up cuz we did not sleep...) Anyways, we began researching about it. The fact we got to know was astonishing. 'It never rains in *Rayli*' Okay, so we got an advantage to explore the forest even when rains. Explore the forest? Wait, we could do that advised Yur. But yeah, we didn't want to die so early. After snacks, we thought of resting in the park.We went there, and sat on the ground. The surroundings were beautiful, the breeze was playful, and the sky was sweet!

we were talking, when suddenly Yur probably saw something so she quickly caught my hand and pulled me out of the park. When I asked her what had occured, she bobbed a no, and said, "*Nahi* Mrunda! How is it feasible? I saw someone hiking around the forest!"

"Shhhh, calm down, you might have likely seen someone, like, a kid playing or something?"

"Nope. It was tall, and it had hair messed up and in front of it's face!"

"Oh, well then, you might have imagined it!"

Come on. I took a grip of her hand and took her home. After the dinner, we went in the basement, in there, we had a box full of great grandpa's stuff. And because he was a monster hunter, we had a demon detector. It was black remote with an antenna, four buttons on it which were labelled as "Detect monster", "Detect spirit", "Maps", "Find a safe place". We silently took it upstairs, changed the battery, and kept it under the bed, so that no one could see it.

In the midnight, we got off for the 'HUNT'. As we were near the parks boundry, we heard a loud scream, and came running. and directly got in the bed. We had been so scared, that we straight away went to sleep. Next morning, when we got down, on the dining table, Yur saw the news paper, and gave me a call. I went there to see the horrifying picture and a journal.

I thought, we should give this a rest day, cuz we had enough of this *Rayli* story. The next day as we reached school, everyone was talking about the news article from yesterday. Anyways, during the last period, I looked of the window, and was thinking of the forest. "Tring-Tring" the bell rang. Later, us walking home from the school, in the sunlight, crushing the berries beneath our feet. We thought of sitting in the park for a while. We took off our bags and sat down. Instantaneously, It started raining. And without thinking of anything, I pulled her towards the forest, as it does NOT rain there. And then, near the border, I percieved we don't have to go there, and as we turned to go back, it pulled us inside. For real it was not raing. As we were trying to get out of here, an invisible wall was stopping us ! At this moment of time, I just sat down holding my head. And Yur started blaming me. We were already in an argument when a fire stone came flying. I pushed away Yur, so that she doesn't get hurt.

While I was jumping aside, the stone hit my leg. It took a piece of my flesh with it. The pain was torturous. It was the moment of realisation, I couldn't lift my leg. Yur got hysterical. She started looking for a rope or something like that so that she could tie me up on her back, and take me to a lake, to splash water on the wound. She found nothing but a creeper, so she used five climbers and braided them to make a rope. She carried me on her back and we got up in search of a lake. But since it was too late, I suggested that we should sleep. She had to climb a tree, as sleeping on the ground would not be without danger for us. We found a tree which was easy to climb, and slept. In the morning, we continued the search. Yur was tired that's why I used be like, walk a few meters, and she used to carry me. Like so, we travelled. Once we were tired, we sat under a tree. We fell asleep. I heard a crunch, and I was jolted awake. To my surprise, my eyes saw a bodyless pair of legs! I woke up Yur, and she screamed, "RUN !!" She took me on her back, and started running. She could not run faster because I was a burden on her back. She tripped over and fell. I asked, please, leave us, to the legs. Amazingly, mr. legs said, " No kids, I won't harm you. What are you two kids doing here, in a dangerous place?" We told him the whole history.

"So, you mean, it does not rain here?"

"Ya, we mean, we have been told!"

"*Haan*, It rains rarely, but when it rains, it showers in the worst way possible. Trees get uprooted, you see lifeless bodies of animals, and what else should be told."

We asked it about the monster, He told us that she was not nearby, but she was roaming, and so it was not safe for us to be moving around freely. He suggested that we get out of there as soon as possible.

"How can we?"

"Oh well, there are challenges that will lead you out of here. But remember, you are not supposed to make any mistakes. One small mistake, and you die!"

II

Beware, or you die!

"What kind of challenges sir? " We questioned him. "Go ahead and you'll get to know." As we walked by, we reached a place, with I remember, sixty five gates. As we entered, we heard an abnormal voice, "Welcome to the death path. Here, you have a total of thirty five gates, and a timer with 2 minutes and 30 seconds set up. As soon as the chime rings, all the gates will start to close. Before the time ends, you have to find out the correct door. Once all the doors cloose, a massive fire will lit up! Good luck!" Yur started screaming, cuz she was afraid. I looked into her eyes and told her not to lose hope. I'm sure we will find a way out of here. I rolled my eyes, and I saw a rock. I picked it up, and thought, 'Bro, what if I start throwing a stone in each of the door?' So I did. I asked Yur to join me. We kept doing this. Until, we realised five of them were still left and the carillon had already started ringing out. We haphazardly ran towards the fourth gate on our right. We were literally blessed to enter the safe gate! Once we reached, an 'Ohhhh myyy goddd' escaped her mouth. I lied on the ground on my back, and prayed to god. After a few minutes of rest, we continued to move ahead. We carried on talking and walking. While we were whispering, I turned around and started teasing Yur, that if the monster comes here, what would she do? "Yur, what will you do?? Cry? Haha! Scaredy cat !!"
"Ohh, Mrunda! Stop it!" And the moment, Yur's expression faded!

She screeched, and ran backwards, and climbed a tree. and, suddenly, I felt a hand on my back! It slowly grabbed my uniform (Ya, uniform. we directly came from school) It pulled me up, by the time I reversed, I had already known who it was. It was the monster! I saw her, and was shocked. She looked somewhat like the ghost of 'The Ring'. Just that, monster looked scarier. "Please leave me! I am sorry! I did not come here intentionally! We're sorry! We're just finding our way out" I requested.

"*Nahi!!!* A nice feast has been arranged for me! How do I loose a better opportunity? Huh? You dumb kid! How dare you enter this forest?! It's Diwali coming up, don't you know? And that other kid who ran away. I am having you, as a good three-day feast!" As she opened her big, big mouth, Yur called out, "Nooo!! Please leave her. Have me instead. I taste better. Wait, I'll come down." She came down running. I immediately, said "Negative, I am guilty, and you should only punish the one who is at fault. Have me, let her go, out of the forest, at home."

"No, I am guilty, I made the mistake! Let her go and have me."

"Awww, love between sisters. Reminds me of my sister. I had a sibling, a younger sister. She was four years younger than me. Her name was Ayisha. We used to live here in this forest. We had a house, a beautiful one, with a red roof, a house near the lake, a wooden swing in the balcony, sound of birds chirping, a pretty view, peaceful house-hold and a loving family of four. It was more than enough for me. The closest member of mine was Ayisha. She was a loving and caring sister. We knew each- other's secret! I cared for her so much, I did not even let her get a scratch. I was the best version of myself when Ayisha was around. A sudden day we heard a bullet . Mumma said it must be a hunter. We ignored, and carried on the work. Once again, and once again. "Boom" "Boom" and "Boom". Father went out, and he saw five men standing in front of the house, with guns and bombs. He came running insinde and told us to hide. But as he was coming, the men shot him. We rushed. My mother, she told us to go and hide below the table. We ran towards the table, and shouted, "*Mumma*, come and hide with us.

They'll kill you too! Please mumma, please!" She smiled at us, and said, "Kids, nothing is happening to me. I Will be always with you. Behind you, watching you and I will always protect you. Take care of Ayish-" They killed her. Ayisha went running to mumma, out of the table. I asked her, Ayisha! What are you doing??? But no. She did not listen. They took her away from me, too. I was left alone below the table, weeping. This is the last thing I remember. I wanted to see them smiling and playing. But not. I could not. And I guess I might have been unconscious, but when I woke up, I found myself below a tree, but not alive. However, my anger is out of imagination. I still remember them-" And the moment, she transformed into a pretty lady. Her beauty, her calmness and her sweet voice. She looked like an angel. I could not believe it for a moment. But within a blink of an eye, she was levitating and she started burning. She was screaming. She was desperate to come out of the fire. She shouted, "You kids melted my heart. I give you twelve to fifteen days to solve the mystery of the medal, take it with you. But to do that, you'll have to complete challenges and solve the treasure hunt. You can also go meet the Great Old Tree, if you need some help. Go, I set you free for the given time!" We tried to ask her about what had happened, but a force pulled us away from there. That area turned the brightest it could. We had been terrified and were sweating a river. I lay down right there. Yur had been thinking about that since she heard it. We were walking, night had already fallen and we found a tree easy to climb, so we got up on the tree, and we were on the opposite branches. I guess Yur had fallen asleep, but I could not.

MEANWHILE - AT HOME :

Nani: *Arreeyyy,* it's been ten days the kids are missing! I want my kids back (weeping)

Yur's Mother(Masi): Mom, Stop crying. It won't change anything. You should have not told it to them. Don't you know? Yur's will to explore the unkown?

Yur's father : I'm sure police must be searching for them, but I did not hear anything from them recently. Let me talk to them...

Nani: But Diwali is about to come...

III

Get! Set! Go! The Journey Begins!

The next morning we set of for the journey. A journey back home. We were really happy, but at some deep part of my mind, I was tensed and scared. How will we complete the tasks in just 15 days? We started moving forward, to most probably, our way back home. Sometime later, we came across an old bridge. Yur tried stepping on it. It made a creaking sound just as if it were to break. It was initially broken. Also we did not have another way to cross. Yur walked on the first plank. Second and third were broken. There were little chances of us surviving! I said, "Yur, hold the rope, and jump over the broken planks." She nodded, and jumped. I closed my eyes. Yesss !! She exclaimed. I looked at her, She was standing upright, in front of me. I tried. It worked for now. We moved ahead and carefully crossed the bridge. On the last plank, I jumped over first, And landed on the ground. When I turned back, I said, "Yur, go on.." She Jumped, she had almost reached the other end, but her leg slipped off, and... I quickly bent over to grab her hand. It was as if she was hanging at the edge of life. I tried to pull her over, but the grip of my hand was too weak to pull Yur up. I saw her falling down. This was the biggest loss for me. I fell on the ground, and tears came rolling down my cheeks. I screamed and cried. Until I heard a sound "Neighhh !!!" I wiped my tears and looked up, to see Yur sitting on a unicorn! I looked at it as it glided in the air. It landed on the ground. And Yur got off it. And turned back to look at the unicorn and thanked it. I ran towards Yur and hugged her. The unicorn made a neigh sound, and gave me a chit. As I read it,

"Oh, already found 1 chit? Don't worry. Just 1 more to go. But Don't celebrate yet. The second one is going to be way more harder...

Where silence kills a man, not much travel through it. Once you find the switch, turn it on and get the second clue.

Options;

The tunnel --> North- west

The Cave --> North- east

Best of luck."

It was a bit easy though. We started moving forward. We thought of visiting the tunnel. So we walked ahead. It was evening already and we were still walking. We had been talking about our journey. While walking, I felt something fall on my shoulder. Oh shit, I said. I looked at it, it was a gross big worm! A big and fat one. OMG. And we started running like anything. One more dropped, and one more. It was like ewwww!! We kept running and we found ruins, of a very old house. Without thinking of anything, we entered the house an sat under the roof. We carefully pulled out those worms. And rested for a while. We started exploring the ruins. Upstairs, it was dusty and broken, but it would have been a beautiful house sometime ago. We found a book shelf. It had a collection of old books, like ' Victoria ' and, ' The secret behind titanic ' And all. I pulled out a book to look at it, but the shelf started moving violently. It broke, and we saw a door. As we went inside, there was a lantern and a box of matchsticks. She lit up the lantern, and saw another door in the room. There was a number lock, and 3 books on the floor, and a chit with "The password is in the bar codes of books" written in it. I took the books, and looked at their bar codes. I thought of entering the first three number of each code, but that did not work. I tried another few patterns, but those did not work either. And then, all of a sudden, the door opened, with a three number digit of the code. We marched in, and saw a beatiful room. It had a collection of antiques, perfumes, etc. I looked in the drawers of the table, and found a map. It marked the ocation of the tree. We decided of moving towards the tree to find out what was it. We hiked forward. But while moving there, we had been hungry, so we started looking for fruits. We saw berries on a bush. We gave it a glance. I plucked out one of it and munched on it. It was very sweet and so I adviced her to eat it. We sat for a while and ate the berries. Yur suddenly held her stomach and shouted, " Ahhh, it hurts." I picked her up and walk forward. I could not carry her for a long, so I put her on the ground and asked her to sleep and I slept. After a few hours when I woke up, I saw a branch of the tree holding Yur. It kept her down, and she was alright. I went to her, and looked up at the tree, and thanked it. I got to know that he was the great old tree, where the monster found herself, not alive, but dead. He bent towards me, and talked to me. He told us that two more challenges were remaining, and one chit had to be found, in which we were given the location of a box, which contained the medal to open the door. He gave us a bag with three water bottles and three tiffin boxes, and a compass and a chit with a mantra, to call him when needed. We thanked him and moved forward. When we were walking, the ground beneath us suddenly disappeared, and fell down, sliding all our way to another challenge. It was a laser trap.

The laser trap

We had to stay away from those, not to touch it. Slowly and carefully, I crossed first. It was easy for me. Then from the other side, I called her out. She did it too, but she was in a hurry, and so she touched the last laser. I quickly took out a bottle from the bag, and poured water on her, cuz her clothes had started burning. And shoot! I did not do it purposely, but I poured water on the laser. I pulled her up as soon as possible, and we ran far from those electrified lasers. We checked if everything we had was alright, and it was.

IV
Yur's Powers

Next up, now we had a compass. We continued treking our way to the tunnel, in the North- west. While moving ahead, I noticed a mark, on Yur's wrist. It looked like a sun- symbol which glowed.

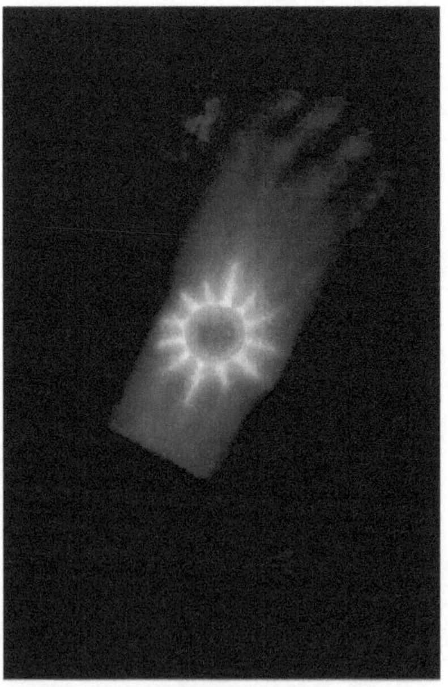

Enter Caption

I asked her about. Even she was shocked, about the mark appearing on her wrist out of nowhere. Unexpectedly, a branch pulled me, up high, very vigorously. In a rough voice, it said, " Arghhh. Got you tiny little human child. Hmmmm... I have not eaten human flesh in decades. I got a chance!" "Wait! Put her down." Yur yelled. She started hitting him, trying to rescue me, so that we would run out of there. "Ohh well well. Trying to act smart? No worries. I can eat that smartness of yours." It grabbed Yur in its branch. She was moving vehementally, to get out of it's snatch. The tree took Yur near his mouth and was about to eat her, when a force pulled Yur out of it's grasp. I never saw Yur, as fierce as I saw her that day. She fell on the ground and started digging the ground. The tree laughed at her, and looked at me. It took me to his mouth, and swallowed me! Yur was digging the ground and she withdrew a dagger out of the ground. I had been suffocated in there. It was about to chew me up! Somehow, I knew that something was up with Yur. She ran with the dagger, straight in the direction of the Tree. It tried to shoo her away, with its branches, but by hook, she dodged its attacks. She frantically stabbed the dagger in the root of it. It spit me out, I took a hold of her hand and ran away from there. " I did not do it consciously." Yur stated. It was the mark who had made her do all of this. "How did you know about the bayonet under ground?"

"Listen, Mrunda, I saw our great grandfather. He told me about everything, like, what do I have to do to save you, and what do I need. I could feel my mark prickling." We did not know anything about the mark. We just carried on forward. While walking, we came across a cave. It was a dark one. We opened our bag, and took out the compass to see if we had been marching in the correct direction. To comprehend, instead of North- west, we moved ahead to North- east. We thought of trying to see once if anything we could find in the cave.

As we set our foot into the cave, magically the cave lit up! It was wonderful! We stepped ahead. In the inside of the cave, was a Diary on a stand, with butterflies around it.

The Diary

I had an urge to just pick it up, and start reading. I headed to get it, and when I moved my hand towards it, it repelled away my palm. "Yur, can you try getting it?" I ask. She moved her hand toward the diary to take a hold of it, and she could. I guess the diary was only meant for her :(

As she read it, I could see her jaw drop a few minutes later. I questioned her. She told me to read it. Simultaneously I read it to find out-

An amazing theory!

Actually, it was that Demon wasn't guilty. She had been turned evil, by another influencing spirit. And all her soul wanted was salvation. She knew the correct person, who would help her do that. There would be two young girls, whose great granfather were a demon hunter. Their family had been blessed by an angel. The blessing was represented by a sun mark on the wrist. And one of them, less blessed has a brown mark on her ankle (which I did). The forest would pull them in the right time, so that they could free her soul, by fixing a badge to the right place, and get a key to the place where they could help her soul get salvation...

V

Salvation to her soul

Now that we had known, that we were the chosen ones, we had to fix the badge, and give her soul, what it craves for- salvation. We did not have to do the challenges, we just had to help her. I felt so bad about her, she did not get her justice. Now it was time for us to help her. Only 6 days had been left.

Yur closed the diary and looked at me. Her face was a mix of shock and understanding — like everything suddenly made sense.

"We're not here to survive anymore," she whispered, "We're here to save her."

I nodded. My heart was racing. "But... how do we find the badge?"

Yur held up the diary and turned to the last page. There, in fine golden writing, it said:

"The badge lies where it all ended — beneath the ashes of the red-roof house. Follow the path of the rising sun. When the sun touches the oldest branch, you'll find the truth."

I looked at her. "The red-roof house... Her old home. We have to go there."

It was clear what we had to do. We packed our bag, took the compass, the map, and the mantra, and set off again.

The journey wasn't easy. The forest began to change — less dark, but not yet light. A strange mist followed us. The sun above, finally visible, became our guide.

After hours of walking, we saw it. The remains of a house, almost hidden beneath vines and time. Red roof tiles lay scattered, half-buried in soil. The old swing still hung from a bent balcony beam.

"This is it," Yur said, voice trembling.

We walked into the remains. It was quiet. Peaceful.

And then the ground trembled.

Suddenly, the ashes beneath the center of the house glowed. A voice whispered: "The badge awaits. Speak her name."

Yur knelt down and whispered: "Meera."

A golden light burst from the earth. Slowly, gently, a round bronze badge emerged from the ground, engraved with ancient markings and a glowing sun symbol.

I held it in my hands. It was warm. Alive.

Just then, a gust of wind encircled us, and we heard a voice — not monstrous, but soft, grateful:

"You found it. Now help me be free."

The wind quieted, and for a moment, the forest seemed to hold its breath. The silence wasn't empty — it felt full, like it was waiting for something to begin... or end.

Yur stayed crouched, her fingers brushing the soft earth where the badge had emerged. Her eyes were distant, focused, like she was listening to something only she could hear.

"She's ready," I said softly.

Yur stood, wiping her hands on her jeans, her face set with quiet determination. "Then we finish what we started. We take it to the altar."

We unrolled the map again, and something had changed. A golden trail now shimmered faintly across the page, winding from the ruins of the red-roof house deeper into the forest. It stopped at a new symbol — a circle wrapped in thorns, with a sun burning at its center.

We didn't speak. We just nodded, and followed it.

The deeper we went, the more the forest changed. The shadows thinned. The mist pulled back, as if making space. The trees no longer loomed or whispered — they simply stood, like old guardians watching us pass.

Time blurred. Hours, maybe. The badge in my pocket pulsed with a steady warmth, almost like a heartbeat. Like it was alive.

Then the trees parted.

It wasn't a clearing in the usual sense. It felt... sacred. Like the forest had pulled back just enough to reveal something it had been protecting for a long time.

At the center stood a stone altar, weathered but strong. Moss climbed up its base. Fireflies hovered in the air like floating embers. Four massive trees bent toward each other overhead, their branches weaving into a canopy that glowed faintly with golden light.

We stepped forward together, quietly.

"This is it," Yur said. Her voice barely carried above a whisper.

I took the badge from my pocket. It felt heavier now, warmer. I placed it on the altar.

As soon as it touched the stone, a soft glow spread outward — not in a burst, but like sunlight stretching slowly across the forest floor. It moved through the roots, up the trees, into the air.

Then, she appeared.

Not the creature we had feared.

Not the shadow that had haunted us.

Just... a girl. A torn white dress hanging from her frame, eyes like sunlight after rain. Her hair drifted gently, suspended like it was underwater. She didn't stand — she hovered, just above the earth.

"Thank you," she said. Her voice didn't echo anymore. It rang clear, gentle. Human.

Yur stepped forward. "Meera. We know your story now. You're not forgotten. You're not alone."

A soft smile curved Meera's lips. "I never wanted to hurt anyone," she whispered. "But the pain... the anger... it twisted everything. I was lost."

She looked at us, and for a moment, she just breathed. "But you brought me back."

She handed over a piece of rock, which carried the same sun carving, like the one on my hand.

Then something shifted — not loud, just... felt. Like the whole forest exhaled.

And from the trees behind her, another form began to glow.

Smaller. Younger.

A child.

Meera turned. Her breath caught. She fell to her knees, hands covering her mouth.

"Ayisha..." she said, barely audible.

The little girl ran to her. Ayisha opened her arms. They collided in an embrace so pure it made the air around them shimmer.

And then light — bright, warm, golden — lifted them both. It wrapped around them like a spiral, rising higher and higher, until it was hard to tell where thcy ended and the light began.

And then... they were gone.

No cry. No crash.

Just quiet.

And sunlight.

The first real sunlight we'd seen since we stepped into the forest.

We stood there for a long time, not speaking. Just breathing. Just feeling.

Then, the badge — now silver, clean, and still — floated gently down and rested on the altar.

Yur stepped forward and picked it up.

"She's free," she said.

And I believed her.

VI
Back Home

The forest didn't feel haunted anymore. It felt alive.

We followed the path back — but it had changed. Flowers grew where there was once ash. The air smelled like rain.

When we stepped out of the forest, the portal appeared glowing gold instead of blue.

We held hands and stepped through.

The sun was setting. Diwali had just begun. Lanterns floated in the sky. Crackers burst in the distance. And our mothers were waiting. This time, they believed us. Or maybe... they didn't need to. Maybe they just knew something had changed.

That night, we lit a diya for Ayisha. And one for Meera. As we placed them on the balcony, Yur whispered:

"Not all ghosts need to be feared. Some just need to be remembered."

The wind gently blew the flames.

The badge sat on our shelf — quiet, peaceful.

Until the night it glowed again.